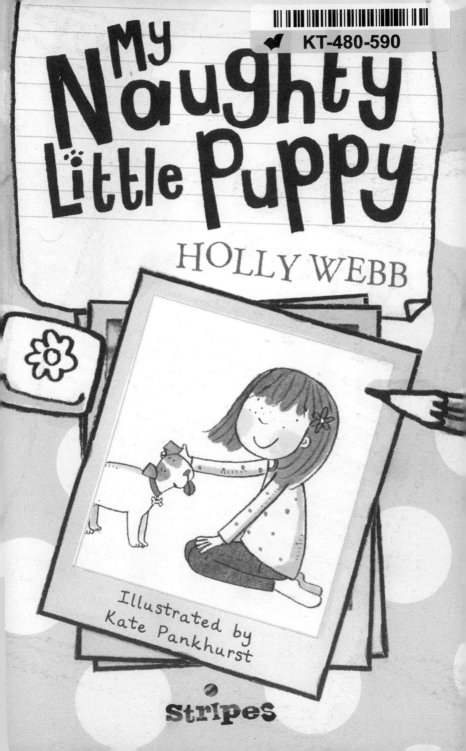

My Naughty Little Puppy

HOLLY WEBB

Illustrated by
Kate Pankhurst

Stripes

Rascal and
the Wedding

Ruff!
Ruff!

For Judith ~ H.W.
For Lauren and James ~ K.P.

Woof!
magazine

STRIPES PUBLISHING
An imprint of Little Tiger Press
1. The Coda Centre,
189 Munster Road,
London SW6 6AW

A paperback original
First published in Great Britain
in 2012

Text copyright © Holly Webb, 2012
Illustrations copyright
© Kate Pankhurst, 2012

ISBN: 978-1-84715-232-9

The right of Holly Webb and Kate
Pankhurst to be identified as the
author and illustrator of this work
respectively has been asserted by
them in accordance with the
Copyright, Designs and Patents
Act, 1988.

A CIP catalogue record for this
book is available from the British
Library.

Printed and bound in the UK.

10 9 8 7 6 5 4 3 2 1

For more information
about Holly Webb visit:
www.holly-webb.com

Chapter One

The Invitation

"Mum, look!" Lila raced into the kitchen, where Ellie and Max were eating breakfast before school. "It's arrived!"

"Is it the invitation?" Mum dropped the clingfilm she'd been wrapping round Ellie's sandwiches, and seized the silvery envelope. "Oh, look, isn't it pretty, with the little flowers woven into the paper..." She eased the envelope open very carefully.

"Gorgeous," Lila said admiringly.

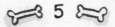

My Naughty Little Puppy

"What is it?" Max asked.

Lila and Mum glared at him. "Auntie Gemma and Liam's wedding invitation, of course!"

Max shrugged. "But we've known about the wedding for ages. Why do we need an invitation? What are you getting so excited for?"

My Naughty Little Puppy

Lila sighed, and Mum shook her head. "It's important, Max. Auntie Gemma's been waiting ages for these to arrive. They were a special order. You know she wants everything to be perfect for the wedding."

Max groaned. "Yes... You never stop going on about it. I'll be glad when it's over. Only another month of wedding, wedding, wedding..."

"Can I see, Mum?" Ellie asked, leaning over to look at the pretty dark pink and silver card. "Ooh, it's got all our names on. 'Miss Ellie Thomas'." She giggled. It sounded very posh. Then she frowned thoughtfully. "It doesn't mention Rascal..."

Lila rolled her eyes. "Ellie! You weren't expecting Auntie Gemma to invite a dog to her smart wedding, were you?" Lila looked over at Rascal's cushion. "Especially not *that* dog..."

Ellie had to smile. Rascal was asleep on his back, with all four paws in the air. His paws twitched every so often, and as she watched he started running in his sleep, his little legs bicycling. "He's lovely!" she told Lila firmly.

"Yes, he's a lovely little *monster*, Ellie! Rascal at a wedding! Just think about it!" Lila folded her arms and stared at Ellie.

Ellie sighed. "I suppose so." She had to admit that Lila was right. Wherever Rascal went, chaos always seemed to follow...

My Naughty Little Puppy

"So when's the wedding?" Jack asked.

"The beginning of May," Ellie
explained. "Auntie Gemma wanted it to be
springtime, but not too cold."

They were waiting for their dog-training
class to start, and Ellie had just been telling
Jack about the wedding – and how Rascal
couldn't go.

"So is it a big smart do, then? Do you
have to wear some pink frilly dress?"

"It's very smart. And I have to go and
try on my bridesmaid's dress next week."
Ellie made a face. "I'm looking forward to
it, but Auntie Gemma didn't know that dog
training is on a Wednesday now, so I'm

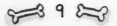

going to have to miss next week's class."

Rascal and Jack's huge Great Dane Hugo had been moved up to the intermediate dog-training classes, which were once a week on Wednesdays. The lessons were slightly more difficult, and some of the other dogs were very clever. There was a German shepherd called Frisky who Ellie thought had been given totally the wrong name. He wasn't frisky at all – he was the best-behaved dog she'd ever seen. Ellie was convinced that if Dan, Frisky's owner, told him to walk up and down the hall on his hind legs holding a dog biscuit between his teeth, he'd do the trick without even licking the biscuit. But Dan was very nice, and he'd told Ellie that Jack Russells were a nightmare to train, and she was doing really well with Rascal. Since Rascal had just shot in front of Dan and tripped him up, it was good of him to say so.

Unfortunately, Amelia and her spaniel Goldie had moved up too, which meant she was still there to make mean comments about Rascal and Hugo all the time. She was waiting for the class to start too, sitting close to them with Goldie on her lap, and a superior look on her face. She had her hair drawn up into a ponytail with a feathery band round it, and she looked far too smart for dog training – she always did.

"I was a pageboy at my cousin's wedding when I was five," Jack told Ellie. "I had to wear this awful blue velvet suit. It was a disaster." He shuddered.

"What happened?" Ellie said anxiously.

"I was supposed to be walking behind my cousin carrying the rings, but she was walking really slowly, and I trod on the end of her dress ... the long train bit. I tripped over and fell on top of the train, and my cousin ended up pulling me down the aisle on it. I kept hold of the rings, though," Jack added.

Ellie laughed, but she couldn't help thinking, what if she did something awful like that?

"You're going to look dreadful in a bridesmaid's dress."

My Naughty Little Puppy

Ellie looked up, her eyes widening.

It was Amelia, of course, with a nasty smile on her face. "You're the kind of person who always wears jeans, Ellie. You'll just look a ratty mess."

Ellie glared at her, and then smiled. "Um, Amelia..."

"What? You know I'm right, Ellie."

"Actually, it wasn't about that. Did you know that Hugo's eating your hairband?"

My Naughty Little Puppy

Ellie had to admit it was quite nice going to a dog-training class where Rascal wasn't the worst-behaved dog for once. Jack's mum took Amelia's hairband to the ladies and washed off the dog-slobber, but Ellie had a feeling it was never going to be the same again. It didn't help that she and Jack kept looking at each other and cracking up all the way through the class.

At least it made the lesson a bit less serious. Rascal was finding the intermediate level fairly difficult. Jo was trying to teach the dogs the same kind of things they'd learned in the beginners course, but they'd all got a bit more tricky. So they'd practise sit and stay, but now the dogs had to stay for more than two minutes.

Rascal's worst bit was the food manners training, when the dogs were supposed to ignore bowls of food, and not beg or jump up if their owners were holding a biscuit. For Rascal, ignoring a food bowl was torture. Frisky and Billy, a Lab who was almost as un-frisky as Frisky, sat gazing at the bowls with angelic expressions, and even Hugo managed not to eat anything, although he did keep standing up and looking hopefully at Jack.

Meanwhile, Rascal had already wolfed down half his crunchies, and stared at Ellie as though she was mad when she took the bowl away.

My Naughty Little Puppy

Ellie sighed. "Maybe you'll be better when Max brings you next Wednesday," she told Rascal. But she didn't feel very hopeful.

DOG Training here

Chapter Two

Making Plans

On Saturday morning, Auntie Gemma came round with Liam to talk about the wedding plans. She brought a huge folder with her full of pictures she'd cut out of magazines, and another with all the details about the church and the hotel where the reception was going to be held. She'd already got her wedding dress, but it was a secret – only Mum had been allowed to see it. Now they had to choose the bridesmaids' dresses.

And Max's pageboy outfit. Ellie had
told him Jack's horror story about the velvet
suit after dog training on Wednesday, and
he was very anti the whole idea of dressing
up. He glared at the folder as Auntie
Gemma opened it up.

"I'm not wearing anything like that!"
Max said in disgust, as Auntie Gemma
spread out some pictures across the table.
He was staring at a photo of a cute, curly-
haired little boy in short satiny trousers and
a shirt with a frilly collar.

Lila picked it up. "Awww! I think you'd
look lovely in that, Max!"

"Never!" Max snarled.

"Don't worry, Max." Liam patted him on
the shoulder. "We were thinking that you'd

wear something more like me and the
ushers. A smart suit, that's all."

"Really?" Max asked suspiciously.
"You promise?"

Auntie Gemma gave a little sigh, and
Ellie had a feeling she'd liked the idea of
Max in satiny trousers. Liam must
have talked her out of it.

"You'll look about sixteen," Liam promised Max. "Really cool."

"OK," Max muttered. "As long as I don't have to do anything embarrassing."

"Anyway, I've got something I know you'll like," Auntie Gemma told him, bringing out a cardboard box from her bag of wedding stuff. "Look! We went to the cake shop earlier and we've got samples for you to try." She moved her folders on to the floor so that she could spread out the different pieces of cake. "There's a fruit cake. A vanilla sponge. Chocolate – you liked that one best, didn't you, Liam? I need you all to help me decide."

Max brightened up, and stuffed a large piece of the chocolate cake into his mouth. "Definitely this one!" he said, spitting crumbs. "Fantastic!"

Ellie nibbled each of the different flavours. "Do we really have to choose just one? They're all yummy."

"I hadn't thought of that. If we have three layers in the cake, we could have more than one sort, I suppose," Auntie Gemma said thoughtfully. "I'm sure I read something about that, in one of my magazines." She reached down for her folder, and squealed with horror. "Rascal! You bad dog! Get off that!"

Ellie gasped, and ran round the table to see what Rascal was doing. Perhaps Auntie

My Naughty Little Puppy

Gemma's folder smelled of food from being in the bag with the wedding cake samples, or maybe Rascal just liked the look of the pretty pink cover. It was now pretty, pink and delicately chewed all round the edges. And Rascal had several cut-out pictures trailing from the corner of his mouth. He was wriggling back from Auntie Gemma, wagging his tail in a sorry sort of way.

Ellie knew that guilty look well.

"I'll take him out into the garden for a run," she said hurriedly, pulling the pictures out of his mouth, and passing them back to her aunt, who stuffed them into the folder crossly.

"I'll come with you!" Max said swiftly.

Ellie shooed Rascal out, and glanced back into the kitchen, where Mum, Auntie Gemma and Lila were bent over the folders with their heads together.

There was no way Rascal was going to the wedding now...

Chapter Three

Dress Disaster

"Make sure he does a wee before you go into the class. And don't let him get too close to Goldie. Amelia won't have forgiven me and Jack for the hairband incident yet, she'll try and get you into trouble. And don't—"

"Ellie! It's only dog training, I'm not robbing a bank. I think I can manage." Max folded his arms and grinned.

Ellie sighed. She still wished Auntie Gemma had chosen another day for the dress-fitting. But hopefully Rascal would behave. "Be good for Max, Rascal!" She crouched down to pat his ears, and Rascal licked her nose lavishly. "Uuurgh. Just do what Max says, OK?"

Rascal looked from her to Max, and back again, and put his head on one side.

Ellie tried not to laugh. It looked as though Rascal was saying, *Really? Do I have to?*

"Are you ready, Ellie? Come on, we need to get going." Mum looked her up and down. "You'd better go and get changed. Those jeans have got muddy paw prints all over them!"

"But I'm only going to take them off and put dresses on," Ellie tried to argue, but Mum was having none of it.

"Run, Ellie! We'll wait for you in the car."

"We're going to be late," Lila wailed.
"And I want to have lots of time to try
everything on!"

Max rolled his eyes. Liam was sorting out
his suit for the wedding, and he'd arranged
to take Max into town nearer the time. Ellie
was starting to think that Max had got lucky.
Lila, Mum and Auntie Gemma in a shop full
of posh frocks might be just too much.

She dashed downstairs five minutes
later in a denim skirt, hoping that Mum
would think she looked OK. Max was
trying to put Rascal's lead on, to take him
for a quick walk before training, but Rascal
was leaping around his feet and barking

like a dog who'd never been near a
training class in his life.

"Sit! Sit, Rascal! Ellie, help!" Max yelled.

"Sorry! Got to dash! Lila's going to kill
me!" Ellie raced out to the car, where she
could see Lila and Mum both looking
impatient.

The dress shop was in a street of smart boutiques. Auntie Gemma was standing outside, looking at her watch and frowning.

"We're not late, are we?" Mum asked.

Auntie Gemma smiled. "Actually you're exactly on time! I was only teasing you."

"Oh, wow..." Lila was staring at the window display. "Look at that gold bridesmaid's dress... And the purple one..."

"I know, they're gorgeous. But we have to get pink, remember?" Auntie Gemma pointed out. She was very strict about her colour scheme.

Lila nodded. "That's OK. I love pink."

My Naughty Little Puppy

Ellie made a face behind her. Lila looked fab in pink – her red hair didn't clash with it somehow, but Ellie's did. Unless it was just the right shade of pink. She really didn't want to end up in a baby-pink dress covered in frills...

The shop assistant had seen them, and was waving them in with a huge smile. "Welcome to Wedding Belles! I'm Fiona. Now, I've laid out some possible bridesmaids' dresses for you to have a look at," she explained to Auntie Gemma.

Ellie could see them, draped on a big purple sofa. They were very pink. And very frilly.

"Your older bridesmaid would look lovely in something a little plainer, like this one."

My Naughty Little Puppy

She held up a smart dark pink dress, without
a single frill, and Lila nodded admiringly.
"And your little one..." Ellie scowled. She
might be younger than Lila, but she wasn't
little. "Something like this...?" Fiona's voice
trailed off doubtfully. Ellie and her scowl
didn't really fit with the ruffly pastel pink dress
she was holding out.

"How about something a little simpler?"

My Naughty Little Puppy

Mum said. "Lila, go and try that one on, while we look for a dress for Ellie."

And that was how it went on. Lila looked more perfect in every dress she tried, while Ellie looked like a grumpy person wrapped in frills. Even Fiona was getting tired after an hour of trying out different dresses. And Ellie felt terrible. She wasn't trying to be difficult! But pink frilly dresses just didn't suit her.

"What about something like this?" Auntie Gemma said, for about the fifth time, waving a page cut out from one of her magazines. She got up from the sofa to pass it to Fiona. She and Mum had been sitting next to a huge pile of dresses that "didn't quite work", and as she stood up, a few pictures slipped out of her folder and fluttered to the floor.

"Oooh! Now *that* could work!" Fiona pounced on one of the photos on the floor – which had a delicately nibbled edge.

"Actually..." Auntie Gemma went pink. She was too embarrassed to admit that she hadn't meant to say she liked that picture, it was just one that she'd stuffed back in the folder after Rascal had chewed it. But Fiona wasn't listening anyway.

"Yes, nice and plain, but with the detail all in the fabric... Lovely! I've got something just like it here." She pulled a dress off the rack. "And it's the right size, too!" She patted Ellie on the shoulder. "I think you'll like this one, I promise."

Ellie eyed it doubtfully. At least it wasn't frilly, but it was covered in flowers! She plodded back into the changing room, passing Lila in another perfect pink dress.

She put on the dress, and looked at herself in the mirror, expecting it to be awful like the others. But actually, it wasn't bad. Ellie took a deep, relieved breath, and twirled round. Nice! It had a fun swirly skirt, and a cool green bow round the waist. She shot out of the changing room.

My Naughty Little Puppy

"Please can I have this one?"

"Oh, Ellie, it's lovely!" Mum said, sounding relieved.

Auntie Gemma nodded. "I hadn't meant to have green in the colour scheme, but it's definitely better than the others..."

Ellie twirled again in front of the big mirrors, holding out her skirts and smiling. Rascal had chosen her the perfect dress!

Chapter Four

Bridesmaid Practice

"Rascal, no!" Ellie howled, as Rascal darted out into the middle of the aisle, leaping impossibly high to seize Auntie Gemma's bouquet in his sharp little teeth. Ellie chased after him, and realized that every single person in the whole church was staring at her and pointing.

She sat bolt upright, gasping, and opened her eyes. Thank goodness it was only a dream! At the end of her bed, Rascal

My Naughty Little Puppy

looked up at her curiously, as though he
was wondering what the matter was.

"I think it's probably a good thing you're
not coming to the wedding," Ellie said
shakily. The dream had left her feeling all
wobbly.

Rascal stood up, and marched along the
bed to nestle next to her, with his head in her
lap. He could tell when she was upset, even
if he didn't know why.

My Naughty Little Puppy

Ellie sighed. It was stupid to be getting nervous about the wedding. It was still three whole weeks away. But she was having nightmares about it already! She *was* going to have to walk down the aisle of the church, and everyone *was* going to be staring at her. Only it wasn't going to be because of her badly-behaved dog...

She put on her school uniform slowly, admiring the dress hanging on the back of her wardrobe door. It really was beautiful. But what if she tripped up halfway down the aisle, like Jack had done? It would be awful if she fell flat on her face in front of everyone.

Mum was in the middle of an urgent phone call with Auntie Gemma – something to do with whether to have salmon as part of the dinner at the wedding or not – so she didn't notice that Ellie hardly ate any breakfast. She ended up running Ellie to school in the car, they were so late leaving.

"Are you all right, Ellie?" Christy asked her, as she trailed in through the playground gates. "You look sort of miserable."

Lucy nodded. "Aren't you feeling well? Oh! How was the dress fitting? Did you find one you liked? Or is that what's wrong?"

"It took ages, but we got a really nice one. I am starting to worry about being a bridesmaid, though. Getting the dress made it all seem real. Everyone's going to be looking at me!"

"They'll mostly be looking at your auntie," Lucy pointed out.

"Not if I fall over and make a total idiot of myself they won't!" Ellie wailed.

"But you won't fall over. You're not having to wear high heels or anything, are you?" Christy asked.

Ellie shook her head. "No, Lila is, but I've got flat ones, like ballet slippers. With a ribbon. They're pretty. I'm just really scared that something's going to go wrong. Last night I dreamed that Rascal ate Auntie Gemma's flowers. It was awful."

"It'll be OK. I'll make sure you don't fall over," Lucy said comfortingly. "You two spent ages teaching me not to be nervous with dogs, so I could be in the dog-food commercial. Now it's my turn. I'm going to teach you to walk nicely, Ellie. We've got

a few weeks before the wedding. Five minutes at break every day, and you'll be a perfect bridesmaid."

Ellie hugged her. "That would be brilliant. Can we start now? There's a couple of minutes before the bell goes."

"OK. Here, hold my water bottle and pretend it's your flowers." Lucy walked around Ellie, pushing up her chin, straightening her shoulders, and generally making her look smart. "Now walk. Fix your eyes on something in front of you. Maybe there'll be a stained-glass window in the church? Head up!"

"I know!" Christy walked backwards in front of Ellie, sticking out her tongue and making silly faces.

My Naughty Little Puppy

"What are you doing?" Ellie sniggered, almost dropping the water bottle.

"You need to practise your 'wedding face' – so you don't get the giggles in the middle of the church," Christy told her firmly.

"Actually, she's right," Lucy agreed.
"If you can ignore Christy looking like that,
you'll be fine with anything. My dance
teacher always says that if you make a
mistake you should just keep smiling and
pretend it didn't happen, and the audience
won't even notice."

Just then, the bell went and they had to
stop. But Ellie was feeling better already, just
from telling Christy and Lucy how she felt.

"I'll keep practising," she promised Lucy,
as they headed inside.

By the week before the wedding, Ellie
could walk across the school playground
like a princess. Even Max asked her if she'd

got taller somehow, and Mum was really impressed when she demonstrated what Lucy had taught her.

"You should show Gran and Grandpa," she said, hurriedly dusting the photo frames on the shelves in the living room with her sleeve. Gran and Grandpa were coming to stay for the wedding, and for a couple of days beforehand. Auntie Gemma and Liam lived in a flat, and didn't have space for them. But of course Auntie Gemma wanted her mum and dad there to help with the last minute wedding preparations.

Mum had already vacuumed the whole house, and then done the stairs all over again twice to get rid of the dog hair. Mum made Ellie help too. She'd had to follow

Mum around with a duster. Lila was holed up in her bedroom with a pile of Auntie Gemma's wedding magazines, and Max somehow managed to disappear whenever there was housework to be done. Then they'd made a cake, and washed all the windows. Gran was quite fussy.

Also, Gran was not a huge dog fan. She liked Rascal sometimes, but only when he was being sweet and well-behaved. They'd gone to stay at Gran's last summer holidays, and Rascal hadn't behaved very well.

"Just don't let Rascal jump up too much, Ellie, will you?" Mum reminded her.

"I promise." Ellie nodded. "He's in the garden. I thought it would be good if he had a run around before they came. I'll go and get him – oh, he's scratching at the door."

There was a determined scrabbling noise at the back door, followed by a couple of demanding yaps. Rascal was good at letting people know what he wanted.

Ellie opened the door, and Rascal stared up at her happily.

He was plastered in thick, smelly mud!

Chapter Five

Fun with Feathers

"What have you been doing, Rascal?" Ellie gasped. "Look at you!" Most of him was brown instead of white, and he smelled awful. "I think he's been rolling in the compost heap," Ellie said, holding her nose.

"Why now?" her mum sighed. "Gran and Grandpa will be here any minute! OK, Ellie. Get him upstairs and give him a bath. Just make sure you leave the bathroom tidy afterwards. And then you'll have to change, too. No, don't let him walk! Look at the pawprints! I'm going to have to wash the kitchen floor again..."

A trail of muddy pawprints led from the back door to Rascal's food bowl. Ellie hurried over to pick him up.

"Oh, I don't believe it, there's the doorbell!" Mum groaned.

Ellie raced upstairs with Rascal. He looked around curiously as they hurried into the bathroom. He didn't go in there very often. But he backed away worriedly as Ellie turned on the taps, and the water spurted out. *Now* he remembered...

"It's OK," Ellie told him. "It's just water. We need to get all that grot off you, and fast. Gran and Grandpa will be wondering

where we are." She could hear Mum saying hello to them downstairs, and Gran's voice floated up.

"There's a very strange smell, dear, are you having trouble with your drains?"

Ellie sighed. "She means you, Rascal. There, that's enough water." She picked him up. "Ooh, Rascal, stop wriggling! Oof!"

A tidal wave slopped over the edge of the bath, as Rascal wriggled out of her arms, and plunged head-first into the water.

Ellie sighed. She was going to have a lot of mopping to do...

My Naughty Little Puppy

"What *is* that silly dog doing?" Gran stared down at Rascal as she came into the living room. She hadn't been too pleased about Rascal sniffing around while she tried to unpack, either.

"Sorry, Gran. I think he likes your fluffy slippers," Ellie explained, shooing Rascal away. Gran had pink slippers, with a feathery trim that wafted about as she walked. Rascal had never seen anything like them and kept following her around. So far, Ellie had managed to stop him snapping at the feathers, but it was hard work.

Everyone was getting a bit stressed out. It was lovely having Gran and Grandpa to stay, but Gran liked everything to be perfect. (That was where Auntie Gemma had got it from.) She kept making "little suggestions" about the wedding that meant Mum and Auntie Gemma had to nip into the garden and panic together.

My Naughty Little Puppy

"I'll put Rascal in the kitchen," Ellie said hurriedly, picking him up. Then she went back into the living room. Grandpa was reading the paper, whilst Mum, Gran and Auntie Gemma tried to work out where everyone was going to sit at the reception. It was like the worst kind of maths homework, where Cousin Suzey couldn't sit next to Great-Aunt Anna, because of What Happened That Christmas, but they both had to sit close to Uncle Gerald. Ellie was supposed to be helping, but it was making her head ache. Eventually she sidled over to Mum.

"Can I take Rascal round to Christy's and see if she wants to go for a walk?" she asked hopefully. "I'll come straight back if she can't."

 51

"Good idea, Ellie," Mum said, without looking up from the seating diagram. "What about if we...? Oh, no, that won't work..."

Ellie tiptoed away, and slipped into the kitchen with a sigh of relief. They'd go to the park with Christy and her dog Bouncer, and just keep out of trouble.

Unfortunately, she was a bit too late. Rascal hadn't been allowed to play with Gran's feathery slippers, but he'd found the next best thing.

Mum's fascinator. The feathery hat-thing she'd bought to go with her purple dress for the wedding. She'd left it in its box on one of the chairs, after she'd shown it to Gran.

My Naughty Little Puppy

It looked very pretty, wrapped round Rascal, as he snoozed on his cushion. The purple feathers set off his brown patches nicely.

Ellie gulped. What were they going to do? Rascal's cushion was scattered with bits of feather, where he'd chewed it. It was ruined!

Ellie snatched up Rascal, and stuffed the fascinator into its box, quickly picking up the feathery bits. The walk would have to wait – she was going round to Christy's on an emergency hat rescue mission now.

"It doesn't look *that* bad..." Christy said, eyeing the fascinator, which was lying on her bed. "Can't you just explain to your mum?"

"No!" Ellie wailed, and Rascal looked up at her in surprise. "She's so stressed, I can't tell her. Please can you help me mend it?"

"I've got a bag of feathers," Christy said. "Mum bought me them for making cards and stuff. We could use those..."

"Thank you!" Ellie hugged her.

"Let's send Rascal back downstairs with Bouncer first," Christy suggested. Rascal was eyeing the fascinator with a bit too much interest. He had a taste for feathers now.

"Have you got purple, to match?" Ellie asked, once they'd left Rascal and Bouncer in Christy's kitchen.

Christy hadn't. But there were some very smart black ones, with a sort of greenish shine to them.

"They do look nice. Mum's going to see that something's happened to it if we use those, though," Ellie said doubtfully.

Christy nodded. "I know. But to be honest, Ellie, she was going to anyway."

"I suppose you're right," Ellie agreed. "OK. Let's fix them on."

Christy had some sequins, too, and they added a pretty scattering over the feathers, carefully gluing them on one by one. By the time they'd finished, Ellie thought the fascinator actually looked a lot nicer. But how was she going to break it to Mum?

My Naughty Little Puppy

"You could just put the fascinator back in the box and hope she doesn't get it out until the morning of the wedding," Christy suggested. "She'll be so busy then, she won't care."

Ellie sighed. "You're probably right."

"What are you doing with Rascal during the wedding?"

"Leaving him at home," Ellie said sadly. "Dad said he'd pop back and take him for a walk before the reception, so he won't be alone all day. I suppose at least there won't be anything important left in the house for him to chew by then."

"Do you want me to pop round and get him just before the wedding? I can look after him, and you can pick him up on Sunday."

"Are you sure? You know what he's like..." Ellie waved at the bits of purple feather all over Christy's bedroom.

Christy grinned. "It's all right. I'll make Bouncer guard him!"

Chapter Six

A Howling Mess

Ellie and Rascal went round to Christy's
house the next day as well. As it was the
day before the wedding, so much was
going on at home it seemed safer to stay out
of the way. But they still had to go to the
church for the rehearsal that evening. Dad
had agreed to take Rascal for a good walk
in the woods close to the church afterwards,
so they could really wear him out. Ellie
wanted him to be nice and tired, so he didn't

make life hard for Christy when she was
looking after him on the day of the wedding.

Ellie had planned to take him for a
long walk on Saturday morning, too, but
when she'd said so, Mum and Gran and
Lila had looked at her as though she'd
grown two heads.

"Don't be silly, Ellie dear," Gran tutted.

"Ellie, you've got to get into your dress!
And have your hair done," Lila pointed out.

"I need you all where I can see you,"
Mum added, grimly. "Not off in the park
getting muddy, or falling in the pond, or just
– well, I don't know."

"Me as well?" Max moaned.

"Definitely you," Mum agreed. "No
going out! I might even bolt the front door."

Dad winked at Ellie. "I don't suppose I..." he began.

"No!" Mum snapped.

"It was just a thought." Dad got up and put an arm round her. "Don't worry. This time tomorrow, we'll all be dancing at the reception."

"Oh, I hope so," Mum sighed. "There just seem to be so many things that could go wrong."

Ellie tried not to look guilty. It definitely wasn't the time to mention the fascinator.

The rehearsal took ages and ages. Ellie could see why it was important – Auntie Gemma and Liam needed to know where

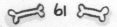

to stand, what to say, and when to say it. But
did it really have to take so long? She'd left
Rascal outside in the churchyard, tied to one
of the benches with his lead, and she hated
the thought of him out there on his own.

It didn't help that the rehearsal was so
serious. She was still a bit worried about
tripping over. Or what if she had a coughing
fit? That would be awful. She felt silly,
walking down the aisle while she was
wearing her jeans. It just didn't feel right.

Gran kept fussing, and worrying about
exactly where the flower arrangements
were going to go the next day, and whether
the church had been dusted properly. But
Grandpa was enjoying himself.

"It reminds me of your mum and dad's

wedding, Ellie. Walking her down the aisle.
I'm really looking forward to it."

"You aren't nervous at all?" Ellie asked.
The church was so big, and there was an
awful lot of aisle to get down.

"No! I know there's a lot of fuss. But it's
a lovely thing, a wedding. Just remember
that." Grandpa bent down to whisper. "And
don't worry about the exact colour of the
lilies, or whether the ribbons on the
garlands are going to be too long.
It actually doesn't matter."

Ellie giggled. She could see why he
whispered. Gran would have told him off.

"Anyway, I thought you walked down
there beautifully just now. Like a little
princess."

Ellie beamed at him. "Thanks, Grandpa! My friend Lucy taught me how."

"Right, now quiet please, so we can practise the vows," the vicar called, and Ellie leaned against Grandpa to listen.

"Do you, Liam Angus Cooper... What was that?" the vicar looked up in surprise. Ellie turned round as she heard the howling, too. She had been thinking that it was an awful long time for Rascal to wait on his own. She'd left him some water and some dog treats, but he was obviously bored. Perhaps he'd stop in a minute...

But he didn't. The barking and mournful howling went on, and Auntie Gemma started looking cross. Ellie hurried out of the church, her cheeks scarlet.

My Naughty Little Puppy

The moment he saw Ellie, Rascal stopped howling and jumped up delightedly.

"Sorry, Rascal, I didn't think the rehearsal would take this long," Ellie sighed, hugging him close. "It was making me feel a bit like howling, too. Do you know, I've been looking forward to being a bridesmaid for months, but now I think I'd rather come and stay at Christy's with you tomorrow..."

Chapter Seven

The Big Day

"Wake up, Ellie!"

Ellie moaned sleepily, as Lila tugged at her duvet, and started shaking her. Rascal joined in with some cheerful morning barking.

Lila never woke up before she did. What was going on? Ellie yawned, and was just about to stick her head under her pillow, when she realized.

Today was the Big Day!

Now she definitely wanted to stick her head under the pillow. She groaned.

"What's the matter?" Lila asked. "Aren't you excited?"

"I suppose so," Ellie muttered.

Lila sat down on the edge of her bed. Rascal trotted up the bed to look too, in case he was missing something interesting. His whiskers tickled Ellie's nose, and she sneezed and sat up.

"What's wrong, Ellie?" Lila frowned. "It isn't the dress, is it? I thought you really liked it."

Ellie shook her head. "I love the dress. It's just – well, everything! I'm scared it's all going to go wrong. What if I fall over and look really stupid? Or my dress gets torn?

Or something else awful happens..." She
wrapped her arms tightly round her knees
and shivered.

"Oh, Ellie!" Lila hugged her. "None of
that's going to happen! It's going to be a
fab day. And you look so nice in that dress,
honestly. We're really lucky being
bridesmaids."

"I know. It's just – you're better at that sort of thing. You don't mind everybody staring at you. When people are staring at me I think it's because I've got my skirt tucked in my knickers. But you know it's because you look gorgeous." Ellie sighed.

"You're going to look gorgeous too," Lila said firmly. Rascal jumped on to Ellie's lap, and buried his cold, damp nose under her chin, making her squeak. "See? He agrees with me."

Gran and Grandpa had gone and bought muffins for everyone to have a special breakfast. But Ellie only picked at hers. For a start, Auntie Gemma kept looking at her watch and making her feel like she needed to eat faster. And she just wasn't hungry.

"The hairdresser will be here in a minute," Auntie Gemma muttered, looking at her watch again. She had a panicky sort of expression on her face, and she was having a hard time sitting still. "Then the florist is bringing the flowers over at about eleven. And we mustn't forget to leave time for some photos. We've got to get it all exactly right..."

"Don't worry, Gemma. We'll just have a sandwich for lunch," Mum put in. "Nice and early, and then we can get you and

the girls into your dresses. What time did you say the car was coming?"

Auntie Gemma smiled and suddenly looked really excited, instead of worried like she'd been a moment before. "It isn't a car! I've been keeping it a secret – Liam doesn't know either. It's a carriage and horses!"

Ellie looked up. "Really? Horses?"

"White ones," Auntie Gemma told her. "With lovely long manes. They looked beautiful on the website."

Ellie brightened up a bit. Rascal might not be coming to the wedding, but the horses sounded wonderful.

"Oh! Don't let that dog anywhere near the shoes!" Auntie Gemma squeaked.

My Naughty Little Puppy

Ellie got up hurriedly to shoo Rascal
away from the pile of
shoeboxes he'd been
sniffing. Rascal
glared at her.
He was sulking.
Everywhere he
went, he seemed
to be in the way.

Ellie patted him gently and rubbed his
ears, but she had a feeling it was only
going to get worse. Looking at the
timetable that Auntie Gemma had typed
out, the whole day was busy, busy, busy.
The house was going to be full of people,
and none of them were going to want a
small, hairy dog around...

My Naughty Little Puppy

"Are you ready, Ellie?" Mum called. "You're going down to the church in a minute."

Ellie was sitting on the sofa, trying not to move in case she messed up her pretty hair, or spilled something on her dress. Rascal had been shut in the kitchen, because he kept trying to jump on her lap. He didn't like the house being full of people, and he wanted Ellie to cuddle him. She just hoped he was all right. He'd whined at the door for a few minutes, but he'd stopped now. He was probably asleep, she decided. Christy would be round to fetch him soon, and he'd be fine playing with Bouncer.

"I'm ready, except for the flowers," she

said, as Mum came into the living room.

"Good. Don't forget to pick them up before you go." Grandad was coming to walk Ellie, Max and Lila down to the church, as it was so close.

Ellie wondered when Mum was going to put her fascinator on. She'd sneaked another look at it while the hairdresser was there, and she thought she and Christy had done a really good job. She just hoped Mum thought so, too.

"I'll get them now, so we can leave as soon as Grandad arrives," she told Mum. Ellie's flowers were in a white box on the cool tiled floor in the kitchen – the florist had said that was the best place to keep them fresh. She could check on Rascal at the same time, but she was pretty sure he was asleep on his cushion.

Ellie crept into the kitchen, not wanting to wake Rascal up. But he wasn't on the cushion as she'd expected. She looked round the kitchen worriedly, and her heart thumped as she realized that the florist's box was half open, the cardboard lid pushed up – and a little chewed.

"Oh, no..." she whispered. She tiptoed across the room, not really wanting to look.

Rascal was asleep – in the box. On top of Ellie's posy of pink flowers. Or what had been a posy. It was squashed flat under a tubby little brown and white dog.

Ellie put her hand to her mouth in horror. What was she going to do? It wasn't like

the fascinator – that had been mendable.
There was no way Ellie could make those
flowers look like something she could carry
down the aisle.

Rascal woke up and panted at her
happily. Ellie picked up the squashed posy,
and stared at it.

Just then, Grandad came into the kitchen. Ellie hadn't even heard the doorbell ring.

"Ellie, are you ready to go to the church?" he asked, and Ellie shook her head. She didn't know what to do.

She dashed past Grandad into the hallway, darting through the open front door and out on to the pavement, where a coach was just drawing up, pulled by a beautiful pair of white horses.

But Ellie couldn't even bear to look. She raced on down the road, searching for somewhere to hide.

Chapter Eight

Max Saves the Day

Ellie was sitting on the bench in the churchyard, the same one that she had tied Rascal's lead to the evening before. It was round the back of the church, so no one would see her. That way, at least she could join in with the wedding again after the church part. It wouldn't matter then if she didn't have any flowers.

Lila would be fine walking down the aisle on her own. Ellie sniffed. The dress didn't have any pockets, and she didn't have a tissue. All she had was a squashed posy of flowers. She looked down at them miserably. Auntie Gemma would be arriving soon. Liam was probably inside the church already – she'd seen a few guests as she'd slipped in the back gate. Mum and Lila and Auntie Gemma were probably wondering where she was, but she couldn't go into the church like this. Auntie Gemma had said everything had to be perfect – she wouldn't want a bridesmaid with squashed flowers.

"Ellie! There you are!"

Ellie looked up in surprise as Max raced towards her in his smart suit, dragged along by Rascal.

"Don't let Rascal jump up at her!" Lila

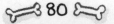

shrieked, as she pattered after him in her pretty heels. "He'll get mud on her dress!"

"It wouldn't matter," Ellie said sadly. "I'm not doing it."

"Ellie, why? What happened?" Grandad said breathlessly. He'd been chasing after Max and Lila. "We had to tell your mum and Gemma you'd taken Rascal round to Christy's. It was lucky Max saw which direction you raced off in."

"And I think Rascal was tracking you, Ellie, he knew exactly where to go," Max put in. "What's happened?"

"Look." Ellie showed them the flowers. "They're all spoiled. I can't walk down the aisle with those, and I have to have flowers!"

"Did Rascal sit on them?" Lila said, sounding horrified.

Ellie nodded sadly. "He went to sleep in the flower box."

"Can't we get some more?" Max suggested. "There must be somewhere..."

Lila shook her head. "There isn't time."

"You really can't use those?" Max asked hopefully. "They don't look that bad..."

Lila rolled her eyes. "Of course she can't. Look, don't panic, Ellie. You can have my flowers. It doesn't matter. Auntie Gemma wants us there, that's what's important."

"Hang on..." Max said thoughtfully. "It said in one of those magazines—"

"You read a wedding magazine?" Lila interrupted, eyebrows raised.

Max shrugged. "They've been all over the house for months. Anyway, they said that it was cool to have a dog at a wedding. Sort of traditional but trendy. Don't look at me like that, Lila, that's what it said. And they had a picture of a bridesmaid carrying a little dog."

Grandad laughed. "Well, it would make sense, as Rascal was the one who squashed the flowers."

Lila looked at Rascal thoughtfully. "Here, Ellie, give me those." She unfastened Rascal's lead, and then took the posy and undid the green satin ribbons (which Auntie Gemma had picked to match Ellie's sash).

Lila tied them neatly around Rascal's neck. "There! He looks really cute."

Rascal snapped at one of the dangling ends, but he did look lovely.

"Do you really think I can carry him in the church?" Ellie asked doubtfully. "Won't Auntie Gemma mind? She was cross about him howling yesterday. What if he does it again?"

Max shook his head. "That was only because he wasn't with you. He'll be fine if you're carrying him."

"Anyway, she hasn't got time to mind!" Lila said suddenly. "Look, there's the carriage! We've got to be waiting for

her at the door of the church, come on!"

Max and Grandad hurried to get inside
the church. Ellie and Lila stood by the
church door, Lila looking perfect in her
dress, with her unsquashed flowers, and
Ellie holding Rascal and feeling worried.

"Oh, wow! She looks amazing!" Lila
murmured, as Grandpa helped Auntie
Gemma down from the carriage.

My Naughty Little Puppy

And she did. Last time Ellie had seen
Auntie Gemma, she'd been in a dressing
gown having her hair done. Now she
looked like a princess in her perfect dress.
The pink bodice matched Ellie and Lila's
dresses, but the skirt was ruffled net, with
little glittering gems scattered here and
there. She was wearing a crystal tiara, and
a long white veil.

Ellie and Lila hurried towards her, and she beamed at them.

"There was an accident with Ellie's flowers," Lila explained. "She's going to carry Rascal instead..."

Ellie held her breath, wondering if Auntie Gemma would say no, but she only smiled. "He looks gorgeous."

Rascal was eyeing the horses. Usually, he refused to believe he was a small dog. Ellie was pretty sure he thought he was the same size as Hugo. And he always barked at bigger dogs he met in the park. But now he was sitting quietly in her arms, looking sideways at these huge white creatures.

"Are you all ready?" Grandpa asked. "It's time to go in..."

Chapter Nine

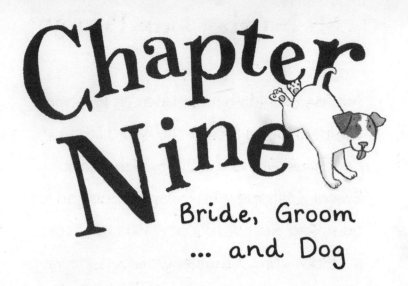

Bride, Groom ... and Dog

As they went into the church, Ellie could hear
a sudden murmur of excitement, and then the
music started. Rascal pricked up his ears,
and glanced round at her curiously.

"Be good!" she told him, as she started
to follow Grandpa and Auntie Gemma
down the aisle, the train of Auntie Gemma's
dress whispering over the stone.

There were delighted gasps and
murmurs as the guests turned to look at

My Naughty Little Puppy

Auntie Gemma – she did look so lovely. But Ellie was pretty sure she heard several people oohing and aahing as she and Rascal went past, and everyone seemed to be smiling. Rascal, for once, was behaving perfectly, sitting still in her arms and showing off his green bow. The vicar was looking a bit surprised, though...

My Naughty Little Puppy

At the front of the church, Auntie
Gemma handed her flowers to Lila, and
she and Ellie went to stand next to Mum.
Ellie gulped. She'd forgotten all about the
fascinator! It looked beautiful, though. The
greeny-black feathers were really striking.

"Ellie, what happened?" Mum
whispered, as soon as they were supposed
to be singing a hymn. "I thought Rascal was
going to stay with Christy..."

Christy! Ellie had forgotten. She looked
worriedly at Lila.

"It's OK, we ran into her on the way to
find you."

"Rascal went to sleep on my flowers,
Mum," Ellie whispered. "They were ruined,
and I got really upset, and..." She didn't

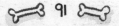

want to worry Mum too much. "It was Max's idea to carry Rascal instead. He saw it in a really smart wedding magazine," she finished hurriedly.

"Well, make sure he behaves!" Mum hissed. "And I need to talk to you about my fascinator, too, Ellie!"

But by the time Ellie and Mum caught up with each other again outside the church after the service, Mum had heard so many people complimenting Gemma and Liam and Ellie on what an original idea it was to bring Rascal, and how beautifully he'd behaved, that she didn't say anything about him at all. Rascal hadn't even minded when everyone threw confetti all over him. It just made him sneeze.

My Naughty Little Puppy

Ellie found Mum talking to her cousin
Suzey, who she knew Mum didn't really
like very much, because
Suzey was always
trying to show off
how glamorous
she was. Mum
was smiling,
though, and as
Suzey moved off
to talk to someone
else, she gave Ellie a hug.

Ellie stared after Suzey.
"Was she wearing...?"

Mum nodded. "The exact same
fascinator that I was. Before you customized
it, that is."

"I'm really sorry, Mum. It was on a chair in the kitchen. You know what Rascal's like..."

"I shouldn't have left it there. But thank goodness I did, Ellie. If Suzey had started going on at me about how much better she looked in that purple fascinator than I did, it would have really spoiled my day!" Mum laughed. "And instead she was looking at mine as if she was jealous!"

"Christy helped me," Ellie explained. "She had some spare feathers and sequins. I wanted to tell you what had happened, but I couldn't find the right time."

"Never mind. And I can't believe how good Rascal's being."

"I know!" Ellie had Rascal on his lead now, and he was sitting beside her looking like butter wouldn't melt in his mouth. "Actually, I think it's because he's scared of the horses."

"Really? Can we get one?" Mum said, jokingly. "Oh, it's time for the photographs."

Ellie hadn't thought that Auntie Gemma would want Rascal in the photos, but when she tried to leave him with Grandad, Auntie Gemma looked round for him.

"Where's Rascal, Ellie? He ought to be in the photos too, he looks lovely and he's been so good."

Ellie gaped at her, but the photographer nodded. "He's a natural. I've already got some gorgeous ones of him in the church. He really adds something special to the photos."

My Naughty Little Puppy

Ellie went pink with pleasure. "He has been in a dog-food commercial," she told the photographer. "He's a bit of a star."

Chapter Ten

Rascal's Lucky Catch

"You'd better not have any more of that cake," Ellie told Rascal sternly. "You'll be sick." She was sitting under the long top table, enjoying a little bit of peace. After the photos, they'd driven over to the hotel for the reception. It looked beautiful – Auntie Gemma had got them to put pink fairy lights all round the hotel entrance, and there were pink flowers on all the tables, and little candles floating in bowls of pink water.

My Naughty Little Puppy

Even the food was
pink – Auntie
Gemma had
chosen salmon for
the main course,
and Ellie was sure it was
because it matched the colour scheme!

She'd enjoyed the meal, and the
speeches – Liam had thanked her and Lila
and Max and even Rascal in his speech.
He'd called Rascal the guest of honour. But
it was late now, almost the time she'd usually
go to bed, and she felt like she'd been on
her best behaviour all day. She needed a
rest, and so did Rascal.

"But you have been very good today,"
she said, stroking his head, as he finished

up the last bit of icing. "You do deserve a
little bit of cake." She peeped out from
under the long white tablecloth, to see
what was going on. "Oh! Auntie Gemma
and Liam are about to do their first dance."

Rascal wriggled in front of her, poking
his head out too. He watched interestedly
as Liam led Auntie Gemma on to the dance
floor between the tables. The band started
to play, and the couple whirled around the
dance floor. Ellie knew that they'd had a
special dance lesson for this, and they
looked wonderful.

Rascal pattered out from under the
table, towards the dance floor, and Ellie
gulped. "Rascal!" she hissed. But he wasn't
listening. He liked Liam and Auntie Gemma

My Naughty Little Puppy

- especially Liam, who had given him some of his salmon from the dinner. He wanted to see if Liam had any more. He trotted on to the dance floor, his tail wagging hopefully. But Liam and Auntie Gemma kept moving around in circles.

Ellie hurried after him to the edge of the

dance floor, a look of horror on her face.
This was a special moment, and Rascal was
spoiling it. But then the band moved into a
faster tune, and Mum and Dad went to
dance too, and Gran and Grandpa, and a
few other couples. Now that it wasn't so
obvious, Ellie hurried to grab Rascal.

Lila rushed after her, laughing. "He looked like he was dancing too, Ellie! It was really cute."

"You think no one minded?" Ellie asked anxiously.

Lila shook her head, and Ellie sighed with relief.

Just then, the band started to play a tune Ellie knew. She caught hold of Rascal's front paws, and started to dance around with him, twirling to the music. She couldn't believe she'd never tried dancing with Rascal before! He was definitely better than Max. Except his paws were a bit muddy. She brushed at the marks on her dress, but they didn't come off. Maybe it didn't matter, this late in the evening.

The dancing wore Rascal's back paws
out, and he was panting with the effort by
the time Ellie carried him back to her chair.
She yawned. The wedding seemed to
have lasted for ages. She'd really enjoyed
it, in the end. But now she wished she could
just find a nice comfy sofa, and curl up on
it. In fact, hadn't there been one in the hotel
reception?

My Naughty Little Puppy

Ellie picked up Rascal – who was sleepy and fat with cake – and went looking for that comfy sofa. No one would mind if they had a little sleep, surely?

The sofa was huge, and she curled up in the corner of it gratefully, with Rascal slumped on her lap. She didn't need to worry about scary wedding dreams any more, she thought, as she dozed off. Rascal had come to the wedding after all – and it hadn't been that bad... And she hadn't fallen over, at least...

"Ellie, wake up!" Lila called.

"What is it?" Ellie asked sleepily, and Rascal yawned and stretched beside her.

"Auntie Gemma and Liam are about to drive off. She's going to throw her bouquet!" Lila grabbed her hand, trying to pull her up.

"What?" Ellie yawned.

"You know! If you catch it, you're supposed to be the next person who's going to get married," Lila explained.

Ellie slowly got to her feet. She scooped up Rascal and followed Lila outside.

Wedding guests were milling around the entrance, and Auntie Gemma was saying goodbye to everyone. She'd changed into a pink suit now, and Ellie realized that she and Liam were about to drive off to the airport. They were staying at a hotel there overnight, before catching a plane to go off on their honeymoon. She was suddenly glad that Lila had woken her – she didn't want to miss saying goodbye.

Auntie Gemma was still holding her bouquet, and as Ellie joined the other guests, she turned round, ready to throw it over her shoulder. Everyone cheered as she hurled it behind her – and a small white dog launched himself out of Ellie's arms to catch the flowers.

Rascal landed neatly, and trotted back to Ellie, the bouquet in his mouth.

"Oh, Rascal!" Ellie looked round, hoping nobody minded. Only Cousin Suzey looked a bit grumpy – maybe she'd been hoping to catch it herself? Everyone else was waving as Auntie Gemma and Liam climbed into their car.

My Naughty Little Puppy

Dad came over to stroke Rascal and give Ellie a hug. "So Rascal's going to get married! Has he met any nice young girl Jack Russells recently?"

Ellie shook her head, giggling. But maybe it meant she could persuade Mum that they should get another puppy...

The Wedding of ♡ Liam and Gemma

photo album

The Holly Story:
All About Holly Webb!

Make no bones about it, Holly Webb is the top-dog author for us! She's written over 60 books, with more on the way. But how did Holly get into writing in the first place?

Holly's first love is books. She loved them so much as a child, that she wanted to be a librarian when she grew up so she could read all day (although that's not really what they do!). Instead, Holly became an editor, which did allow her to read lots of books, and help writers bring their stories to life.

Photo copyright © Nigel Bird

That experience got Holly into writing herself – her company needed someone to write a new series about triplet sisters. So she secretly started writing a book each day on the train to work... She eventually showed it to her fellow editors, and they liked it so much, they published it!

Holly adores animals, and that's why they keep on finding their way into her stories. She has a pet cat called Marble, and has owned dogs, too. Some of Holly's stories are inspired by real life, whilst some just magically appear in her head!

Holly has very messy handwriting. Sometimes she finds it difficult to read her own notes!